MW01078023

THE BIGGEST SMALLEST CHRISTMAS PRESENT

Harriet Muncaster

G. P. Putnam's Sons

Clementine lived in an ordinary house on an ordinary street with her ordinary mom and dad and brother, Charlie.

But there was one extraordinary thing about Clementine . . .

She was the smallest girl in the world!

She was so small, she had her baths in a teacup.

And her bed was made from a matchbox.

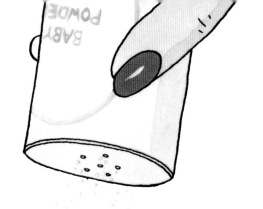

Most of the time, it was fun to be tiny . . .

Sadly, Christmas morning was not one of those times.
Santa brought her nice presents . . .

But they were very BIG.
It was time for Clementine to tell Santa
that she was not an average-sized girl.

"We could make Santa a giant gingerbread cookie and use icing to write that you are a tiny person," said Mom.

"Good idea!" said Clementine. "He can read the cookie before he eats it!"

Clementine spent all day making Santa a big, beautiful cookie. Then she went to bed and dreamed of all the tiny toys he would bring.

The next morning, Clementine woke up and the cookie was gone! A puppy waited for her by the fireplace. A very big puppy.

"Santa's never going to know how small I am!" wailed Clementine.

Over the year, Clementine grew, but not enough to hold the puppy's leash.

The next Christmas Eve, it snowed.

"Perfect!" said Charlie. "Clementine can write Santa a message in the snow on the roof. He'll see it when he lands his sleigh!"

But the next morning, when Clementine came downstairs, there was a shiny new paint box waiting for her by the fireplace. A very big paint box!

"It must have snowed again in the night," said Mom.

Over the year, the whole family thought very hard about how to tell Santa how tiny Clementine was. And just before Christmas, they came up with a plan.

Dad printed out lots of pictures of Clementine playing with the toys Santa had left her, and hung them over the fireplace.

"You did have quite a lot of fun with them," he said.

"Yes, I did," agreed Clementine.

On Christmas morning, Clementine went downstairs
and found a huge package waiting for her by the fireplace.
This Christmas present was the biggest one yet.
"He's done it again!" cried Clementine.
"Oh, dear," said Mom and Dad.
"Let's open it anyway," said Charlie, who loved opening presents.

"Oh, my!" said Mom.
"Goodness!" said Dad.
"Wow!" said Charlie.

In front of them all stood the biggest, most beautiful dollhouse any of them had ever seen. And it was the perfect size for Clementine to play in.

Dear Santa,

Thank you for all the gifts, but especially for my new house! It is the perfect present for me!

Lots of love,

Clementine

X

For Henrietta, Emerald, and Fudge

G. P. PUTNAM'S SONS
an imprint of Penguin Random House LLC
375 Hudson Street
New York, NY 10014

Copyright © 2016 by Harriet Muncaster.
Penguin supports copyright. Copyright fuels creativity, encourages diverse voices, promotes free speech, and creates a vibrant culture.
Thank you for buying an authorized edition of this book and for complying with copyright laws by not reproducing, scanning, or distributing
any part of it in any form without permission. You are supporting writers and allowing Penguin to continue to publish books for every reader.

G. P. Putnam's Sons is a registered trademark of Penguin Random House LLC.

Library of Congress Cataloging-in-Publication Data is available upon request.

Manufactured in China by RR Donnelley Asia Printing Solutions Ltd.
ISBN 978-0-399-16432-3
1 3 5 7 9 10 8 6 4 2

Design by Marikka Tamura.
Text set in P22 Morris.
The images were created using pen and ink and painted
using a mixture of watercolor and acrylics.